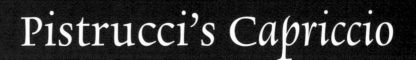

Pistrucci's *Capriccio*

A REDISCOVERED MASTERPIECE
OF REGENCY SCULPTURE

SIR JOHN SOANE'S MUSEUM & WADDESDON MANOR

Pistrucci's Capriccio: A Rediscovered Masterpiece of Regency Sculpture
An exhibition at Sir John Soane's Museum, London, from 1 February to 18 March 2006
and at Waddesdon Manor, Buckinghamshire, from 29 March to 29 May 2006

Published in Great Britain 2006
by Sir John Soane's Museum

Reg. Charity No. 313609
www.soane.org

Text © Carlo Milano, 2006, except where otherwise indicated
Photographs © Mike Fear, Waddesdon, The Rothschild Collection (Rothschild Family Trust), unless otherwise indicated

ISBN 0-9549041-2-5

*Designed and typeset in Albertina by Libanus Press, Marlborough
Printed by BAS Printers, Salisbury*

*Front cover, back cover, title page: Benedetto Pistrucci, the Capriccio, 1829 (detail). Waddesdon, Rothschild Collection (Rothschild Family Trust)
Contents page: Benedetto Pistrucci, self-portrait. Wax. Museo della Zecca, Rome*

CONTENTS

Exhibition curated by Carlo Milano

Catalogue edited by Marjorie Trusted

PREFACE

When the Soane Museum thought of the idea of an exhibition devoted to Benedetto Pistrucci's work and in particular his marble *Capriccio* I could not have been more delighted. Furthermore, the exhibition will travel to Waddesdon Manor and this extraordinary, mysterious, object stands in many ways as a paradigm of the two institutions themselves. Like the *Capriccio*, both are exceptional, intriguing, multifaceted and through the eponymous Soane and Baron Ferdinand de Rothschild, the creations of highly talented, singular individuals. Both are perhaps not as widely known as they deserve to be. In recent years, much work has been done towards the better understanding of Soane and Baron Ferdinand and their legacies, but the *Capriccio*, made by an artist at the height of his powers as an expression of personal turmoil and anger with the establishment, remains an enigmatic work of art in which interest has grown through being lost to public view for over 100 years.

This exhibition will help to dispel the mystery, and the fact that the sculpture can now enjoy the attention it deserves is due to the timely intervention of the export licensing review process which prevented its disappearance abroad and gave an opportunity for its acquisition and public display by a Rothschild family charitable trust – an excellent example of how the system can work for the public good.

Not only does the exhibition cast a fresh light on a neglected subject, but it has created an opportunity for collaboration between Waddesdon and the Soane, and I would be delighted if it were the first of many.

LORD ROTHSCHILD

FOREWORD

The re-emergence of the *Capriccio* of Benedetto Pistrucci in a London saleroom in early 2004 must be accounted as one of the major rediscoveries in British sculpture in the last decade. We are therefore fortunate to be able to exhibit this beautiful and mysterious work at Sir John Soane's Museum, the first time it has been displayed to the general public since it was shown at the Royal Academy Spring Exhibition in 1830.

Strangely enough, despite their mutual interests in sculpture, numismatics and antiquity, and their being contemporaries, we do not know if Soane knew Pistrucci. There are no records of Pistrucci ever having visited Soane's House-Museum, and no works by Pistrucci – medals, cameos or sculptures – are to be found amongst Soane's encyclopaedic collections. Nor was Pistrucci a member of any of the institutions that Soane supported, although the sculptor did exhibit works at the Royal Academy of Arts in 1830 and 1832, where the elderly Soane must have seen them as he was also an exhibitor. Soane was certainly interested in medals and carved gems – when in Paris in 1819 he purchased a set of medals commemorating the victories of Napoleon's reign, arranged by baron Dominique-Vivant Denon for the Empress Josephine, while in 1834, Soane acquired, for £1,000, over three hundred carved gems from the celebrated collection of the 2nd Marquess of Buckingham at Stowe. This collection of ancient and modern gems had been formed from two distinguished Italian cabinets, that of the Braschi, the family of Pope Pius VI, and that of Monsignor Capece Latro, Archbishop of Tarentum. Soane was very proud of this acquisition, which added a new and princely dimension to the proliferating treasury he had established in Lincoln's Inn Fields, so it seems curious that Pistrucci, the most skilful gem-cutter then working in England, and himself an Italian, was not invited to admire and appraise them. But by this time Pistrucci, having alienated his employers and supporters alike by his quarrelsome nature and dilatory working methods, was immured in the Royal Mint, doubtless sulkily contemplating his amazing autobiographical *Capriccio*. In his twilight years Soane could be just as prickly, so one wonders what they would have made of one another!

What is certain is that Sir John Soane would have appreciated the *Capriccio*. At first glance a confused heap of exquisitely carved Antique fragments, it can now, thanks to the discovery of a tiny hermetic inscription, be deciphered as a sculptural manifesto, epitomising the sculptor's personal and professional frustrations. So it is with Soane's remarkable House-Museum, where the architect's own arrangements of classical antiquities and casts, modern pictures and sculpture and architectural models, as well as Soane's own *Capriccio*, his recently recreated *Pasticcio*, form an autobiographical commentary on Soane's interests and enthusiasms, his successes and mortifications, and his strong views on the relationship between architecture and the allied arts.

This small display of Pistrucci's masterpiece and related works is in the tradition of Soane Museum exhibitions on sculpture – such as the recent shows on Flaxman (2003) and Banks (2005) – but it also provides us with an opportunity to look again at a rare and specialised, and largely forgotten, artist of Soane's era. Indeed, Pistrucci's own very distinctive contribution to the Regency age was noted by that elegant, but now alas, unfashionable, writer, Sacheverell Sitwell. In the final, evocative, chapter of his influential book, *British Architects and Craftsmen* (1945), Sitwell imagines a visit to Carlton House in 1812; the magnificent architecture, furnishings and upholstery, the splendid attire of the women and soldiers, 'the bright yellow curricles'. 'Everything is bright and new, and we enter into the spirit of the long summer morning. Putting a hand into our pocket, we pull out the new coins of the reign, fresh from the mint. They are the shillings, half-crowns, and sixpences of Pistrucci, the great Roman gem-engraver. The head of George the Fourth is a miracle of the art of the lapidary, with its crisped hair through which the wreath of laurel winds…'.

Wreaths of laurel are due to all who helped make this exhibition possible. At the head of this list must be our principal sponsor and lender, the Lord Rothschild, whose trust purchased the *Capriccio* in 2005 and ensured that this remarkable work of sculpture remained in this country. Lord Rothschild readily agreed to our suggestion that Pistrucci's *Capriccio* be first exhibited in context at Sir John Soane's Museum, and then at Waddesdon Manor, before it goes on permanent display there and at Spencer House. Thanks are due to the staff at Waddesdon Manor – Pippa Shirley, Colette Warbrick and Vicky Darby – who helped us plan and put this exhibition together. Our thanks also to Mr John Hill of Jeremy Ltd – who bought the *Capriccio* in July 2004 – who also made a contribution towards the costs of this exhibition.

We are especially grateful to Carlo Milano, who curated this exhibition and wrote the greater part of this catalogue, all at very short notice. His enthusiasm for Pistrucci was supported by sage advice given by the distinguished historian Signora Pirzio Biroli who wrote the introductory essay on Pistrucci, which embodies much new material hitherto unavailable in English. Marjorie Trusted edited this catalogue and made a major contribution to the essay on the *Capriccio* – again at very short notice. We thank her for her enthusiasm, professionalism and patience. Especial thanks are due to our other lenders, who agreed to lend works by Pistrucci in a spirit of exceptional co-operation and generosity. They are, in alphabetical order: the Marquess of Douro, the Fitzwilliam Museum, Mr Alan Irvine, the National Portrait Gallery, the Royal Mint, and a private collector.

Finally, much of the burden of administering and mounting this small but impulsively arranged exhibition has been borne by William Palin, Exhibitions Curator at the Soane Museum. My thanks to him to for doing so with such skill, efficiency and good nature.

TIM KNOX
Sir John Soane's Museum
January 2006

Benedetto Pistrucci, Capriccio, 1829 (detail of inscription).
Waddesdon, Rothschild Collection (Rothschild Family Trust)

A ROMAN ARTIST IN LONDON
Benedetto Pistrucci cameo engraver, medallist, and sculptor

In 1829, when he carved the *Capriccio*, Benedetto Pistrucci was 46.[1] He had arrived in London from Rome in 1815 and achieved great success with his cameos, coins, and medals. In 1828 he had finally received the official recognition from the Royal Mint that he had long coveted, becoming Chief Medallist. He had every reason to rejoice: his works were internationally acclaimed, Dominique-Vivant Denon describing his gold Sovereign as 'the most beautiful coin in Europe'. But in reality the late 1820s and the 1830s were unhappy years for Pistrucci, despite the prestigious commissions and the honorary appointments from the main Academies. He was vehemently attacked, in the press and elsewhere, for his position at the Mint and for the delay in delivering the dies for the Waterloo Medal, ordered in 1819 and for which he had already received a large payment, and for the medal for the Royal Humane Society. In 1831 he refused to copy a bust of Queen Adelaide by Chantrey for the Coronation medal of William IV. As a consequence, William Wyon, Chief Engraver at the Royal Mint, designed both faces of the medal. Moreover, he was alone after the return of his family to Rome in 1824, and often ill – Camillo, the only son to remain with him, having recently left to train in the Roman workshop of Thorvaldsen. The elements of the *Capriccio* are a clue to his feelings: he represents himself in chains, bearing the weight of his sorrows 'in the saddest years of my life'. This self-portrait was already known through a wax model, but its presence in the *Capriccio* explains the reasons for such an unusual image and helps us to date the portrait.

The behaviour of Pistrucci is not a surprise because it is coherent with his personality: enterprising and with a strong will, gifted with great talent, but also immodest, temperamental, intolerant, and with a persecution complex. The short fragment of autobiography published posthumously in 1867 by his doctor and friend Archibald Billing and the letters sent to his family in Rome give clear indications of this.

Pistrucci's bad and frequent eyesight problems worsened his mood and in some periods forced him away from his beloved engravings in cameo and metal. His illness, he said, was one of the many reasons for the 30-year delay in delivering the dies for the Waterloo Medal, in 1849, when the political relationship with France had completely changed. He began sculpting in marble to remain active and created the bust of Wellington (1832–1833), the

Self-Portrait of 1835, the bust of Pozzo di Borgo (1839–1840), of Cartwright (1842), of Billing (1845) and of other sitters. Some sculptures today are untraced, especially the Magdalene of 1840 with the portrait of his beloved daughter Elena that meant so much to him: 'I finished a Magdalene more beautiful than all other Magdalenes'.[2]

In Rome, Pistrucci, who in 1800 won the first prize for sculpture at the Scuola del Nudo, studied with the painter Stefano Tofanelli and trained in the art of gem engraving under Giuseppe Mango, and then with Giuseppe Cerbara and Niccolò Morelli, member of the Accademia di San Luca and author of the best portraits of Bonaparte. But he never accepted them as his masters and boasted that he learned all by himself ('…what I have done so far is all work of my brain, I did not have any teachers'), something partially true if one thinks of the boldness of making the dies for the Pound 'without any direction, without ever having the chance of seeing an engraver at work'.[3] He admits the mistake of making those dies in relief instead of engraving them, but adds that with his great skill he corrected them immediately.

Rome was clearly becoming too small for him. His stay in 1812 at the Florentine court of Elisa Baciocchi had not been a success because of the presence there of the Roman Giovanni Antonio Santarelli, the Grand-Ducal engraver of cameos. At this time unscrupulous Roman dealers were exploiting Pistrucci by selling as antique his unsigned works.

The decision to travel to London in 1814, with a short stop in Paris during the 100 Days when he had the opportunity of portraying Napoleon from life, was taken with enthusiasm and determination. Perhaps Pistrucci did not even imagine, despite his hopes, the success that he would find so rapidly in Britain. Initially, his patrons were Sir Joseph Banks, Lady Spencer, William Wellesley-Pole (Master of the Royal Mint from 1814 to 1823) and, most significantly, the secretary to Lord Elgin, William Richard Hamilton, who would be his life-long friend and support him in both his professional and personal difficulties, defending him in the aforementioned press campaign. Later, another mentor was Gladstone, who liked to write to him in Italian while apologizing for his mistakes (1843).[4] When Master of the Mint, he was almost embarrassed to be unable to order new works from Pistrucci until he had completed the Waterloo Medal.

Many of these patrons appear in the extraordinary gallery of portraits by Pistrucci in cameos and wax models, almost all from life and often yet to be identified, now mostly in the sculptor's archive in the Museo della Zecca in Rome. In these models, perhaps more than in the marble busts, we see Pistrucci as an excellent portraitist. His great talent is more evident in these works of small size, in the *pietra dura* cameos (he never used shell) and in the dies for coins and medals. The models made in his first years in London for the new coinage are extraordinary and one can understand the stir caused by his audacious and innovative St George riding naked as one of the horsemen from the Parthenon frieze (so radically different from the traditional heraldic motives of the past). The portrait of George III taken from a coin by Marchant is perhaps not impeccable, but those of the Prince Regent as a Hellenistic Prince (for a cameo, for the Laudatory Medal, and for the medal that was never struck for the acquisition of the Elgin marbles) and of George IV for the Pound and the Coronation Medal are wonderful and masterly interpretations of the finest Greek coinage.

The supreme technique is the same used for his best cameos, like the Medusa in red jasper or the many Bacchic Masks, or the famous Payne Knight Flora. The latter was the subject of heated polemics that would lead him to sign his works with his full name. Too proud of his own work, he certainly did not try to pass it off as an antiquity (contrary to what is still to this day being repeated). Pistrucci cut his cameos from wax models that represent different phases, from the sketch to the final *modello* ready to be translated to stone or metal. The ability to use the qualities of the stone, always chosen with great care, and

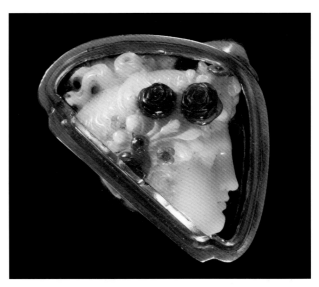

Benedetto Pistrucci, Cameo with the Head of Flora, British Museum, London, from the collection of Richard Payne Knight

the different shades of colour of its layers, with some details carved almost in the round, is the main element in his cameos. The careful and expert polishing, a trademark of Pistrucci that we do not find in other cutters, intensifies the quality of the cutting.

Several works by Pistrucci that were listed as missing in my 1989 monograph have since resurfaced. In particular some cameos, although the large example carved on both faces representing Victoria as Princess and as Queen to which he devoted much time and attention between 1840 and 1841, hoping that Prince Albert would buy it as a present for the christening of the Princess Royal, is still to be rediscovered. After the acquisition of a large group of wax models, the collection of the Museo della Zecca in Rome now includes almost all the pieces left by Pistrucci to his family in 1855.

The newest recovery is the *Capriccio*, surely one of his most significant and problematic works, closely linked as it is with the human and artistic story of its author as well as forming the bridge between the small size cameos and medals and the large size marble sculptures.

LUCIA PIRZIO BIROLI STEFANELLI

The Princess Victoria cameo by Pistrucci on sardonyx c.1836 (Courtesy of The Cambridge Collection)

1 On Benedetto Pistrucci (1783–1855), see L. Pirzio Biroli Stefanelli, *I Modelli in Cera di Benedetto Pistrucci, Roma, Museo della Zecca*, monografia *Bollettino di Numismatica*, I, II, I, 1–2, Rome, 1989.
2 The letters quoted here will be published with the complete correspondence and some new documents in a volume (III, *Addenda et Corrigenda*) dedicated to Pistrucci, edited by the author.
3 Letter sent by Pistrucci to his son Federico from London, 25 October 1833.
4 See note 2

PISTRUCCI'S SCULPTURE

'I have finished a Magdalene more beautiful than all other Magdalenes, today I have modelled it and tomorrow it will be cast, and I hope that before I have to pay for the plaster and the maker of the moulds it will be commissioned in marble and I will receive money in advance for the tears that it has made me shed.'[1]

Pistrucci wrote this in a letter to his wife on 12 June 1840, having just modelled a clay figure of the Magdalene in preparation for what he hoped would be a commission for a marble figure.[2] His words provide a revealing portrait of the man and the approach he took to his art, evoking the pride, ambition and sentimentality that both energised and dogged his career. Like many other sculptures by Pistrucci, no versions of the Magdalene survive, although the 'beautiful model' (presumably plaster) and the unfinished marble are jointly listed as lot 82 in the 1855 sale catalogue of Pistrucci's studio contents after his death. This catalogue, along with Pistrucci's surviving sculptures, provides a basis for exploring his sculptural output.

Although Pistrucci showed an early talent for sculpture, winning First Prize for the discipline at the Scuola del Nudo in Rome in 1800 when he was just 16,[3] there is no evidence to suggest that he produced any large-scale sculptural work in marble prior to the *Capriccio* of 1828–9 (cat. no. 1). His early career as an engraver of cameos and gems does however directly relate to his later output as a marble sculptor, and he had displayed an interest in sculpture as early as 1798. While recovering after being stabbed by a fellow pupil at the workshop of the gem-cutter Giuseppe Mango, he taught himself to model in wax, and a year later he spent some months at the Accademia del Disegno making clay figures, possibly after the Antique. During his time in Rome (*c.*1794–1814), he would have had ample opportunity to see the other sculptors at work, and he was certainly in contact with the sculptor Vincenzo Pacetti (*c.*1745–1820).[4] Although few other works of the imagination in marble by the artist seem to have survived, blocks of marble are listed in the posthumous sale catalogue of Pistrucci's studio contents, as well as 'a beautiful model of a Magdalen . . . the work partly executed in Carrara marble' (lot 82), and 'a shell ornament, in marble' (lot 80). In a letter to *The Times* of 15 October 1838, Pistrucci's friend and supporter W. R. Hamilton noted that the artist had two workshops 'for his private works in marble . . . within the walls of the Mint'.

Pistrucci's early interest in sculpture is not enough to explain the genesis of the *Capriccio* and his specialisation in marble carving from about 1830 onwards. Little work has been done on this later period in Pistrucci's life, although Lucia Pirzio Biroli Stefanelli has put together the most complete list of his sculptures to date,[5] to which can be added a number of untraced pieces from the 1855 sale catalogue. Putting together a catalogue raisonné of Pistrucci's sculptures is nevertheless problematic. The location of a number of sculptures mentioned in early sources is unknown; indeed many may not have survived. One which probably exists, but is as yet untraced, is a bust of Sarah-Bonnetta Davies (Princess Dahomey), the young black godchild to Queen Victoria, mentioned in a letter in the archive of the Royal Mint. It was recorded as being in a private collection in the USA ten years ago, but it has not been possible to re-trace it in time for the publication of this catalogue, and no photograph of it is known.

Pistrucci's works were also on occasion replicated. This is the case with his bust of Wellington (cat. no. 2). Pirzio Biroli Stefanelli lists six marble busts of the Duke, although

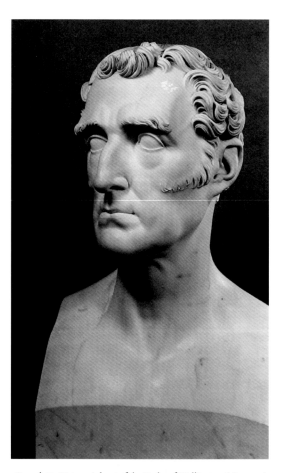

Benedetto Pistrucci, bust of the Duke of Wellington (1832–33). Marble. Apsley House, London (Photo V&A)

some may in fact be mistakenly recorded twice. There are certainly three versions extant: an over life-size bust at Apsley House, and two life-size ones, at the United Services Club in London, and at Stratfield Saye, Berkshire respectively. One of the life-size busts may be that recorded by Waagen in the collection of William Richard Hamilton, an acquaintance of Canova, and a lifelong friend of Pistrucci, in 1854, and the other, the 'Bust of the Duke, life-size' mentioned by Pistrucci in a letter.[6] It has not been possible to verify if yet another replica is still in the Landesbibliothek in Weimar, where it was noted by Thieme-Becker in 1933.[7] Two further works related to the surviving busts of Wellington were listed in the posthumous sale of Pistrucci's works: 'A Mould of the late Signor Pistrucci's fine colossal bust of the late Duke of Wellington' (lot 50), and 'A small bust in plaster of the late Duke of Wellington' (lot 58), both of which are missing today, although we know that W. R. Hamilton bought the plaster bust at the sale (see Appendix, p. 22).

The 1855 Sale Catalogue of Pistrucci's Works

The previously unstudied catalogue of the sale of Pistrucci's studio contents held by Messrs Foster and Son at 54 Pall Mall in London on 30 November 1855 is a crucial document in assessing the artist's sculptural career (see Appendix). As well as a number of marble pieces it lists some of his tools. One, 'a sculptor's . . . bench with a three-screw power to raise six tons, designed and manufactured under the supervision of the late signor Pistrucci', illustrates the artist's technological inventiveness (he had also designed and made machines for making coins). But perhaps the most valuable aspect of this catalogue is the number of moulds, plasters and unfinished marbles listed, which throw light on his work as a sculptor, and tantalisingly refer to works subsequently lost.

Pistrucci was clearly indebted to classical sculpture, and this must derive in part from the twenty years he spent in Rome. Many of the items in the catalogue relate to antiquity. As well as listing two antiquities – 'a fragment of an ANTIQUE GREEK marble bust' (lot 49) and a 'marble cuirass, from Athens' (lot 71) – the catalogue contains several moulds after the Antique, including one of the fragment of the Greek bust, part of lot 49. Moulds of the Elgin Marbles (the Recumbent Theseus, the head of a Horse, and a relief, lots 66–69) are particularly interesting, as they are likely to have been used by Pistrucci in the production of the wax models for the medal commissioned to celebrate the acquisition of the sculptures from the Parthenon by the British Museum in 1816.

About a third of the items listed relate to sculpture which was unknown until the catalogue's discovery, such as the moulds for a bust of the opera singer Madame Pasta, and for one of the Princess Dahomey (lots 52 and 56). Other untraced pieces include 'an original model of a female figure of Thetis, designed for supporting classical drapery'. This may have been a life-size figure of the goddess, perhaps related to the figure of Thetis from the Parthenon, made in the round and used for drapery studies.

The catalogue also helps our understanding of Pistrucci's known works through its listing of related items. For example, Pistrucci made a bust of the violinist Niccolò Paganini (mentioned in a letter of 1832) for the Town Hall of Genoa.[8] The bust has disappeared, but the sale catalogue lists a mould of it (lot 51). The bust of Count Carlo Andrea Pozzo di Borgo, dated 1840, in the Père-Lachaise cemetery in Paris is the only known bust by Pistrucci in bronze. Di Borgo, who died in 1842, was Russian Ambassador in London from 1835, a friend of Wellington and an indefatigable opponent of Napoleon. The sale catalogue lists two related items, (both now lost): a mould, which may have been used during the casting of the bronze, and a marble version (lot 79).

Two plaster models record Pistrucci's competition entry for the Nelson Monument in Trafalgar Square. He exhibited a model for the monument at the Royal Academy in 1839, but no visual evidence of this ambitious attempt to win a major public commission has survived, and the only descriptions are by those critical of the scheme. One critic called Pistrucci's the 'oddest' of the schemes proposed, '. . . undeterred by the miniature work of his general practice, Pistrucci proposed a colossal trident, 89 feet high, rising from a segment of a globe on which three reclining Victories were carving memorials of the hero'. It would be 'nothing more nor less than a large toasting fork'.[9] Another commentator described the monument design as '. . . all prongs and handles standing like a great fork in the middle of Trafalgar Square'.[10] A surviving wax relief in the Museo della Zecca in Rome shows *The Death of Nelson*, a scene that was depicted in a bronze relief by C. E. Carew on the South face on the base of Nelson's Column.[11] Perhaps the wax too was related in some way to Pistrucci's competition proposal.

Other works in the catalogue can be tied in with known works. A plaster mould of the *Capriccio* is listed (lot 55), along with a full-length figure of George IV (lot 63), almost certainly plaster, and probably that exhibited at the Royal Academy in 1832, and the 6 foot 6 inches high plaster bas relief of Thetis and Achilles (lot 64) (also probably shown at the RA in 1839).[12]

A number of busts remain to be discovered, including a 'bust for the wife of a great banker' recorded in a letter of 1833,[13] the original version of Pistrucci's self-portrait (1835), a bust of the artist's daughter Elena Pistrucci (1839), a 'bust for Mrs Morrison', probably the wife of J. W. Morrison, Deputy Master of the Mint, recorded in a letter of 1833 from Pistrucci to his son Federico,[14] a bust of Archibald Billing (1845), and the 1851 bust of a man sold at auction in 1980 (possibly Sir Gilbert Blane, the personal doctor of George IV and William IV).[15] The model for a monument to Wellington in Glasgow (probably an entry in the 1841 competition won by Carlo Marochetti) is also missing.

Pistrucci's later career and his production of marble sculpture

There were many reasons for Pistrucci's decision to turn to sculpture late in his career. One factor was certainly his restlessness and desire for new challenges. Another more practical reason must have been his deteriorating eyesight, which would have made working on the microscopic details of cameos and medals increasingly difficult. In addition the artist needed to develop a new way of generating income. In 1828 William Wyon had been appointed as Chief Engraver at the Mint, and Pistrucci's position there, which had already been weakened by the departure of his mentor William Wellesley-Pole in 1823, became more vulnerable. After his early success and rapid promotion Pistrucci now found himself in a hostile environment and open to public censure. His long delay in delivering the Waterloo Medal, and his overblown neo-Baroque competition design for the Nelson Monument (a long way from the measured celebration of Railton's winning design) were all seized upon by his critics. Executing portrait busts as private commissions was a pragmatic way whereby he could continue to make a living as an artist.

The identification of the sitter of a portrait bust, sold at auction some 25 years ago, with Sir Gilbert Blane, personal doctor of George IV and William IV, remains uncertain.[16] Evidence of the existence of another sculpture that we cannot identify today comes from a photograph of Pistrucci taken by W. R. Hamilton in 1853. The artist holds in his hands a small bust, probably a model, mounted on a half-column.[17]

Pistrucci's busts are almost all herms. This neo-classical style was almost certainly largely due to the influence of Thorvaldsen. The marble is generally highly polished, a feature that in conjunction with careful carving of the details may come from Pistrucci's experience as an engraver of cameos. He concentrated on the formal aspect

of the portrait, rather than a psychological interpretation of the sitter. Interestingly, many of the men who sat for Pistrucci either knew him personally, like for example Archibald Billing, or had a connection with Wellington and his circle. We still, however, know little about the circumstances of the commission of the busts.

Camillo Pistrucci

The sculpting tradition was continued by Pistrucci's son Camillo (1811–54).[18] When his mother returned to Rome in 1824, Camillo stayed in London, where he may already have been working with the father. At the age of 18 he left England with a letter of introduction to Bertel Thorvaldsen (1768/70–1844), and began work in his Roman studio shortly afterwards. Camillo continued to work extensively in Rome, also receiving commissions from British clients. He carved a marble portrait of William Richard Hamilton in 1834, now in the British Museum. In 1841 the wife of Sir James William Morrison, Deputy Master at the Mint from 1801 to 1850, commissioned him to make a replica of the portrait bust of Sir James originally carved by Benedetto in 1839, although this was never produced. Benedetto's original bust is now lost. Camillo also executed a signed and dated bust of Pope Pius IX in Rome in 1848 formerly in the collection of the Duke of Roxburghe (London, private collection, unpublished).

1 'Ho fenito una Madalena più bella di tutte le Madalene, oggi l'ho formato e domani si getta e speriamo che prima di pagare il gesso e il formatore sia ordinata in marmo e riceverò somma in acconto per asciugare le lacrime che mi ha fatto fare.' Autograph letters I, 9. Cited in Pirzio Biroli Stefanelli 1989, I, p. 38.

2 Pistrucci later wrote that the face of his Magdalene was modelled on his beloved and faithful daughter, Elena. ibid., loc. cit.

3 Pirzio Biroli Stefanelli 1989, I, p. 8.

4 Ibid., loc. cit.; idem 2003, p. 467.

5 Pirzio Biroli Stefanelli 1989, I, pp. 36–40.

6 Pirzio Biroli Stefanelli forthcoming.

7 Thieme-Becker XXVII, p. 113.

8 Mostra 1955, p. 25; Pirzio Biroli Stefanelli 1989, I, p. 37. See also cat. no. 7.

9 The Art Union Journal, 1839, p. 18.

10 The Literary Gazette, 1839, p. 343.

11 Pirzio Biroli Stefanelli 1989, I, p. 139, II, no. 107.

12 Graves 1906, p. 156, no. 1309.

13 Pirzio Biroli Stefanelli, forthcoming.

14 Mostra 1955, p. 25; Pollard 1984, p. 46, n. 16d.

15 Christie's London, 16 July, 1980, lot 73; Pollard 1984, p. 46, n. 16; Pirzio Biroli Stefanelli 1989, I, p. 39.

16 Christie's London, 16 July, 1980, lot 73; Pollard 1984, p. 46, n. 16; Pirzio Biroli Stefanelli 1989, I, p. 39. The bust is signed and dated 1851.

17 Pirzio Biroli Stefanelli, 1989, vol. I, plate 8d.

18 Pirzio Stefanelli, 'Di Camillo Pistrucci Scultore Romano', Strenna dei Romanisti, 2000.

THE CAPRICCIO

This is without doubt a capriccio, and that of the most uncommon kind. A block of marble has been chiselled, by a most masterly hand, into subjects without any connection with each other . . . But, indeed, the affair defies minute description as much as it does criticism.[1]

Pistrucci executed only a few marble sculptures, almost all of which were busts, with the important exception of the *Capriccio*. This marble is a personal statement, with specific references to his own life, which by the end of the 1820s had embraced great achievements, but also severe disappointments. It epitomises his professional and personal frustrations, and at the same time marks a high point of his creative powers.

The *Capriccio* was rediscovered recently, having been known previously through its mention as an exhibit at the Royal Academy in 1830, no.1167, as 'Capriccio, in an unfin-

ished state, from a solid piece of marble' by 'B. Pistrucci Chief Medalist [sic.] to His Majesty. Royal Mint'.[2] In 1855 the marble was owned by Henry Labouchere: in the posthumous sale catalogue of Pistrucci's effects, a mould of the *Capriccio* was listed as lot 55, described as 'A mould of the late Mr. Pistrucci's beautiful work, in the possession of the Right Hon. Henry Labouchere, known as the Capriccio'. The mould was unsold, and its current location is unknown. Henry Labouchere MP (1797–1869), a Whig politician and art collector, was Master of the Mint from 1835 to 1841, and lived at Stoke Park just outside Windsor,

Benedetto Pistrucci, the Capriccio, *1829, Waddesdon, Rothschild Collection (Rothschild Family Trust)*

Benedetto Pistrucci, the Capriccio, *1829, Waddesdon, Rothschild Collection (Rothschild Family Trust)*

near Pistrucci's home, after the artist had left London. Labouchere had a taste for contemporary sculpture; he owned for example works by Canova and Thorvaldsen. It is not clear how he came to own the *Capriccio*, but it is possible that Pistrucci sold or gave it to him while he was Master of the Mint. The marble's whereabouts are unknown from 1855 until June 2004, when it was sold at Christie's London from the collection of Professor Jack Robert Lander (1921–2003).[3]

The sculpture appears to consist of separate fragments joined together, but is in fact carved from a single block of marble. It is an intricate piece, with two main faces, and smaller carvings at the sides. A hole drilled into the underside serves as a fixing point for a dowel, but may have been used to allow the sculpture to rotate. The mould listed above in Pistrucci's sale could have been made for the purpose of reproduction, although no copies are known.

More probably it formed part of his working process: the marble was probably based on a preliminary clay model, from which a mould would have been taken, so that a plaster version could be made, to be used as a working model for the final piece. Elements of the piece seem to have been derived from wax models, and from Pistrucci's designs for coinage.

The front consists of three overlapping medallions showing profile heads (one of which is George IV), surmounting a lion's head, which is flanked by a further medallion with the profile head of another male portrait (unidentified, though possibly Pistrucci himself, or perhaps the Rt Hon. John Charles Herries MP, Master of the Mint from 1828 to 1830); this head faces Cerberus in high relief, nose to nose. On the other side of the lion's head is a relief of the head and torso of a reclining naked woman, probably intended as a portrayal of Venus, lying in aban-

Benedetto Pistrucci, Venus. Wax. Museo della Zecca, Rome

don on some drapery, beneath caged beasts. A broken capital supports the medallion of George IV. The other two medallions depict a faun-like man and, at the apex of the composition, an ideal female classicising head. A naked putto, carved in low relief, and probably unfinished, is propped up against the Cerberus. Beneath the lion's head is an incised inscription in small capital letters: 'ROYL MINT/ PRIMO ESERCIZIO/ DI BENEDETTO PISTRUCCI/ NEGL'ANNI I PIU INFELICI DI SUA VITA 1829' (Royal Mint. First trial by Benedetto Pistrucci. In the unhappiest years of his life 1829).

The back of the piece shows a nude figure of Hercules in relief, seen from behind, seated on blocks of stone covered with his lion-skin, and clasping a club in his left hand; part of an oak tree is visible to his left. To the right of this figure, near his left arm, is a separate relief of a man in contemporary dress, stepping outwards, his head bowed. The opposite edge of the relief of Hercules, at right angles to the oak tree, is carved as a vertical frieze, with a butterfly, a skull, a sprig of wheat, and sculpture tools, including a mallet. At the side of this narrow frieze is a nude male figure in high relief, standing cross-legged, his arms above his head, supporting like a caryatid the underside of the medallion of George IV, this underside being carved with stylised clouds. A chain is fixed to the wall at the feet of the man, although he appears to be unshackled. This figure is a self-portrait of the artist, and corresponds with another wax model (see page 3) in the Museo della Zecca in Rome.[4]

The review of the Royal Academy exhibits for 1830 in the *Gentleman's Magazine*, cited at the head of this essay, noted, 'This is without doubt a *capriccio*, and that of the most uncommon kind. A block of marble has been chiselled, by a most masterly hand, into subjects without any connexion with each other . . . But, indeed, the affair defies minute description as much as it does criticism. The female figure is very lovely.' As this contemporary account implies, interpreting the meaning of this complex piece is not easy, and is indeed probably impossible, since it is a work apparently arising from the artist's own discontent, as the inscription makes clear. Formally it recalls Pistrucci's time in Rome, where excavated and restored classical marbles were to be seen, evoking a heroic past, and where artists such as Piranesi were constructing their own fantastic *capricci* made up of classical elements. Pistrucci knew both Canova and Thorvaldsen, and was fully aware of the revival of classical forms in contemporary marble sculpture. The *Capriccio*'s fragmentary, classicising quality may also have been inspired by the Elgin marbles, which had been put on public exhibition in London in 1808, and were acquired for the British Museum in 1816.

The significance of individual elements, and the overall meaning of the whole, is problematic. The artist portrays himself as a heroic nude, supporting the reigning monarch; the man in contemporary dress apparently exiting on the other side could also be a self-portrait. The unidentified male portrait is shown uncomfortably close to Cerberus's heads, perhaps a vengeful gesture on the part of the artist. The lion on the front might symbolise England, while the

Benedetto Pistrucci, the Capriccio, *1829, showing the self-portrait of the artist. Waddesdon, Rothschild Collection (Rothschild Family Trust)*

heroic image of Hercules on the reverse could embody Pistrucci's classical roots in Italy.

Parts of the piece are visibly unfinished, for example the man in contemporary dress and the putto. The description of the piece when it was exhibited at the Royal Academy in 1830 'in an unfinished state', and the inscription on the marble suggests this is a study, 'primo esercizio', rather than a completed work. But these features may be a playful deception on the part of the artist, rather than to be taken literally. The phrase 'primo esercizio' could also refer to that fact that this is Pistrucci's first essay in marble sculpture. Although this piece had serious resonances for the artist, it must also have been in part a witty virtuoso exercise on the nature of sculpture and its purpose, its medals or medallions intermingling with heroic and classical images. Unlike most other sculpture of the early nine-teenth century in Britain, such as the work of Flaxman and Chantrey, this is a medium-scale piece, to be displayed on a piece of furniture, similar in that respect to French *morceaux de réception*. The medallions are larger than the medals Pistrucci normally produced, but the whole resembles an assemblage of disparate, small-scale pieces of sculpture. These illusionistic and fantastical qualities, seldom seen in marble, and its layers of enigmatic meanings, give this sculpture an outstanding importance in Pistrucci's *oeuvre*, and indeed in European sculpture.

Pistrucci had been enormously successful after arriving in Britain in 1815. Within two years he attracted a number of influential patrons and supporters, created the new coinage of the Kingdom and was acting as Chief Engraver to the Mint, although as a foreigner he could not be given the title. His cameos and medals were highly sought-after,

Benedetto Pistrucci, the Capriccio, *1829, Waddesdon, Rothschild Collection (Rothschild Family Trust)*

his coins considered masterpieces. But by the mid-1820s things started to change. In 1823 his friend and staunch defender William Wellesley-Pole retired from his position as Master of the Mint. In 1824 his wife and children (with the exception of his son Camillo) left for Rome. Pistrucci also began to experience problems with his eyesight. In 1828, not long before the marble was carved, he was appointed to the newly-invented post of Chief Medallist at the Mint, his former deputy William Wyon being named Chief Engraver, but each was paid £350 per annum, instead of the £500 salary normally due for the post of Chief Engraver. On 23 July 1829 Pistrucci wrote to John Charles Herries, then Master of the Mint, protesting against what he felt was the unfair treatment of himself as against Wyon.[5] Moreover, he may also have feared that his 'promotion' to Chief Medallist would herald his complete removal from the Mint. He had many enemies, and the slow progress of the Waterloo Medal, commissioned in 1819, had become a new source of criticism. In 1829 Camillo too left him for Rome where he entered Thorvaldsen's workshop. These disappointments and fears, combined with an existing propensity for swings of mood, and a persecution mania, appear to have brought Pistrucci into a state of deep anxiety and depression. The *Capriccio* was therefore produced as an artistic translation of this state: a mid-nineteenth-century representation of melancholy. The word *Capriccio*, used from the beginning as the title of the sculpture and chosen by Pistrucci himself, seems to have been inspired by Piranesi, who used the word to describe his romantic confections of antiquity, redolent with a melancholy sense of abandonment and desolation. Thus the self-portrait on the *Capriccio* shows the artist, in an Atlas-like posture, bearing the sorrows of the world on his shoulders (and perhaps suffering under the unattainable greatness of the ancients), whilst Cerberus and the skull are visions of death. He is also bearing the weight of a portrait of George IV, a reminder of his unhappy artistic association with the King. Following criticism of his early royal portraits for coinage, Pistrucci was instructed to copy those of Lawrence and Chantrey in 1821 and 1822. He refused on both occasions.

In the context of the professional difficulties of 1829, the *Capriccio* can be interpreted from another perspective. By this time, owing to problems with his eyesight, Pistrucci was finding it difficult to work on medals and cameos. This, combined with a general feeling of alienation at the Mint, may have led him to begin sculpting in marble. The *Capriccio* appears therefore to have been the first exercise in this new career, and Pistrucci must have decided accordingly that it should display all his talents. The object would

be unusual, and the composition clever and complicated, through which he could show off his knowledge of antiquity and his superb skill in carving. In fact he worked on the details on the surface of the *Capriccio* with the same attention and precision that he would have used in a cameo.

The possibility that Pistrucci donated the *Capriccio* to Henry Labouchere after he became Master of the Mint (1835) adds another fascinating twist to the story of the sculpture. Pistrucci, frequently attacked by the press for his temper, for the delays with the Waterloo Medal, and for his financial situation, may have thought that he could find support in Labouchere.

The profile of George IV has close links with many other representations of the King by Pistrucci, particularly the wax models now at the Museo della Zecca, although it also has parallels with the cameo from the Fitzwilliam Museum (cat. no 10).[6] The half-length reclining Venus is derived from a wax model representing the entire figure of the goddess in the Museo della Zecca in Rome.[7] The lion's head is also known from two wax models from Rome, and is ultimately derived from Canova's tomb of Clement XIII Rezzonico in St Peter's.[8] The seated Hercules is a quotation from a detail on the obverse of the Waterloo Medal, with some small variations (cat. no. 4).

The *Capriccio*, a miniature compendium of Pistrucci's work up to 1829, would later become a source of inspiration for the sculptor's daughter Maria Elisa, who copied the round medallion with a profile of Flora in her double marble roundel (cat. no. 14).

The *Capriccio* continues to hold our attention whilst evading exact interpretation. It provides a beguiling insight into Pistrucci's personal struggles and artistic achievements. As an Italian artist active in Britain, he brought Italian sensibilities to traditions of English portraiture, and his work in marble and gemstones confirms his mastery of these materials. His artistic achievements reached heights of excellence, and this surviving example of his figurative work in marble adds a further dimension to the study of his life and work.

1 *The Gentleman's Magazine*, Vol. C, Part 1, 1830, p.543.

2 Graves 1906, p. 156, no. 1167.

3 Christie's London, 10 June 2004, lot 76.

4 Pirzio Biroli Stefanelli, II, no. 236.

5 *A collection of letters, etc. from newspapers and magazines, on the respective merits of B. Pistrucci and W. Wyon as medallists*, London, 1837–8 (British Library; Rare Books)

6 For the wax in Rome see Pirzio Biroli Stefanelli, II, no. 42.

7 Ibid., no. 272.

8 Ibid., no. 382.

CATALOGUE

1 **Benedetto Pistrucci (1783–1855)**
Capriccio, 1829

White marble, height 320 mm, width
385 mm, depth 215 mm
Signed and dated: 'ROYL MINT/ PRIMO
ESERCIZIO/ DI BENEDETTO PISTRUCCI/
NEGL'ANNI I PIU' INFELICI DI SUA
VITA 1829'
Waddesdon, The Rothschild Collection
(Rothschild Family Trust)
Literature: *The Gentleman's Magazine*, June
1830, vol. 100, p. 543; Graves, 1970, p. 156,
no. 1113; Pollard, 1984, p.26; Pirzio Biroli
Stefanelli, 1989, vol. I, p. 36; Marsh, 1996,
p.39; Christie's, London, 10 June 2004,
lot 76.

The *Capriccio* is the first sculpture by
Pistrucci, made in 1829 and exhibited
the following year at the Royal Academy.

For a more complete discussion of the
Capriccio, see the essay in this catalogue
(pp. 11–15).

1

2 **Benedetto Pistrucci (1783–1855)**
Bust of the Duke of Wellington,
1832

White marble, height 535 mm
Inscribed on the left: 'XVIII IUN.
MDCCCXXXII XVII ANN. P.V.
WATERLOO', and on the right:
'BENEDETTO PISTRUCCI ROYAL MINT'
The Marquess of Douro, Stratfield Saye
Literature: Billing, 1875, p. 208; Wellington,
1901, II, p. 448; *Mostra* 1955, p. 25; Gunnis,
1962, p. 306; Avery, 1975, p. 39; Pollard,
1984, p. 26; Pirzio Biroli Stefanelli, 1989,
vol. I, p. 37; Marsh, 1996, p. 40.

Pistrucci executed more than one example
of this portrait. Three versions are known
today: the present bust, one at Apsley

House, and another at the United Services
Club, in London; a fourth may be in the
Landesbibliothek in Weimar, but this has
not been confirmed. Contemporary
references mention what may be two
further versions, although they could be
identical with those mentioned above (see
the essay on Pistrucci's sculpture pp. 8–10).
Additionally a plaster bust, about 20 cm
high, was recorded in Rome with the heirs
of Pistrucci (Pirzio Biroli Stefanelli, 1989,
vol. I, p. 133, n. 2).

The first bust in the series of portraits
of the Duke of Wellington by Pistrucci is
the over life-size version in Apsley House,
a mould of which appears as lot 50 in the
1855 auction catalogue (see Appendix).
The Duke sat for Pistrucci on 18 June 1832
(Waterloo Day), and the bust was finished
after sixteen months, during which the
artist worked 'as long as my legs could bear
my body, and my eyes didn't close from
exhaustion' ('finché le gambe potevano
sostenere il mio corpo e fino che gli occhi si
chiudevano') (Pirzio Biroli Stefanelli, 1989,
vol. I, p. 133). When the bust was ready,
Pistrucci, always ready to show off his
technological expertise, had a machine

made to his own design to lift the heavy
sculpture safely. The present Stratfield Saye
bust is a slightly smaller replica of that at
Apsley House. It is of high quality, and is
normally displayed on its original red
marble pedestal, inlaid with a small white
marble relief representing a scene from the
battle of Waterloo. As on the bust of Samuel
Cartwright (cat. no. 7) and on most of his
sculptures, Pistrucci added the words 'Royal
Mint' to his signature.

Pistrucci was in contact with Wellington
and his circle soon after his arrival in
London in 1815. William Wellesley-Pole,
brother of the Duke, was the Master of the
Mint who appointed Pistrucci to produce
the new coinage, and who commissioned
him to make the Waterloo Medal. His
departure from the Mint in 1823 marked the
beginning of Pistrucci's difficulties there.

The artist also portrayed the victor of
Waterloo in three cameos (Pirzio Biroli
Stefanelli, 1989, vol. I, p. 30, nos. 77–79),
a wax (Pirzio Biroli Stefanelli, 1989, vol. I,
p. 135, no.101; vol. II, no 101) and a medal
(see cat. no. 5). Additionally Raffaele
Pistrucci, Benedetto's son, made some
shell cameos of the Duke.

2
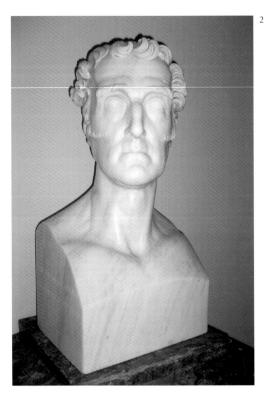

3   Benedetto Pistrucci (1783–1855)
Original Dies for the Waterloo Medal, 1849

Iron, diameter 134 mm
Signed on both dies 'PISTRUCCI'
The Royal Mint, Llantrisant
Literature: *Numismatic Chronicle*, XII,
1849–1850, pp. 115-122; Billing, 1875,
pp. 101-102, 193–194, 205, 210, pl. 143–144;
King, 1872, II, p. 450; Grueber, 1891, pp.
125–126, no. 552; Azzurri, 1887, pp. 9-14;
Parkes Weber, 1894, pp. 113–114, no. 186;
Forrer, 1906, pp. 14–17; Hocking, 1910,
pp. 207–210; Pratesi, 1921, pp. 91–95;
Historical Medals, 1924, p. 78, no. 290,
pl. 84; *Mostra . . .* , 1955, pp. 60-62;
Vermeule, 1964; Balbi De Caro, 1971, p. 13,
n. 23; Valeriani, 1972, p. 39; Avery, 1975,
p. 37, pl. 5; Kent, 1978, pp. 59–61 pl. 24;
Jones, 1979, pp. 104–105; Brown, 1980,
pp. 208–212; Pollard-Mauri Mori, 1981,
p. 24; Pollard, 1984, p. 43; Eimer, 1987,
p. 133, no. 1067, pl. 29; Pirzio Biroli
Stefanelli, 1988, p. 38 ff.; Pirzio Biroli
Stefanelli, 1989, vol. I, pp. 97–103; Marsh,
1996, pp. 23–5, 48–57.

The Waterloo Medal is probably the most famous work to be designed by Pistrucci, and a masterpiece of medallic art. It was however never struck, partly because of Pistrucci's extreme dilatoriness, and partly because of the technical difficulties involved in striking such a large piece. This is the first time that the dies have been exhibited.

In 1816, following the victorious battle against Napoleon the previous year, the Prince Regent proposed that a medal be struck. Four copies were to be issued in gold for the rulers of Britain, Austria, Prussia, and Russia, and two in silver, for Wellington and for General Blücher, Field Marshal of Prussia. Pistrucci was chosen for this task in 1819, and a fee of £2,400 was agreed, to be paid in instalments. This sum was later raised to the exceptionally high figure of £3,500. Pistrucci considered that the work was equal to that required for 30 medals, which normally cost £100 each. As on other occasions, he refused to copy models prepared by other artists, in this case drawings by John Flaxman. Many details of the reverse however are clearly indebted to the British sculptor, as well as to the Parthenon marbles, which had been first exhibited in London in 1808, and which Pistrucci knew well.

In 1822 the Master of the Mint, William Wellesley-Pole (Wellington's brother), informed George IV that the work was already well advanced, and that £1,700 had been paid to the artist. However ten years later, in 1832, the work was still far from complete, and the then Master of the Mint, Lord Auckland, remonstrated with Pistrucci over the delay, refusing to give him any assurance that his contract with the Royal Mint would continue after the delivery of

the Waterloo Medal. A further decade after this, in 1842, the new Master of the Mint, William Ewart Gladstone, who greatly admired Pistrucci, and with whom he spoke Italian, denied him any new commissions until after the Waterloo Medal was completed. Gladstone did however raise Pistrucci's salary from £300 to £350 in 1844, and indeed offered him £400 if he could complete the medal. He began working on the medal again after leaving his house at the Royal Mint and moving to Old Windsor with his daughters later that year.

The dies were finally delivered on 1 January 1849, 30 years after the contract had been signed, but were never hardened. This was a great disappointment to Pistrucci, who had made each of them in two separate parts (a roundel in the centre surrounded by a ring) in order to make the process of hardening easier, in preparation for the striking of the medal. He also wrote an essay in the *Numismatic Chronicle* (XII, 1849–1850, pp. 115–122) with his suggestions on how the striking should be undertaken. However there was little incentive to produce the medal: by 1849 all the protagonists of the battle had died, except for Wellington; in addition political relations between France and Britain had radically changed.

In a letter to W. R. Hamilton of 1 February 1850, Pistrucci describes his feelings: 'I have nobody in the world to whom I can tell my frustrations. It was not by chance that I wrote my name under the thread cut by Fate [this is an allusion to the position of his signature on the medal under one of the Fates]. I knew that this was going to happen after the completion of the medal . . . I have done more than my duty, the villains will triumph over me for a brief time, and I hope that one day their names will be covered in shame . . . My daughters are looking after the dies of the great medal one way or another to make sure that they don't rust. I swear that I have not looked at them for more than six months because I don't have the strength to do so. They have ruined my good health, and they are the cause of all my troubles' (Pirzio Biroli Stefanelli, 1989, vol. I, p. 98).

3

4 Benedetto Pistrucci (1783–1855)
The Waterloo Medal

Electrotypes, diameter 140 mm
Signed on both dies 'PISTRUCCI'
The Royal Mint, Llantrisant
Literature: see previous catalogue entry.

The Waterloo Medal was never struck, but electrotypes were produced after the dies were delivered in 1849. Reduced versions of the medal were also produced in gold, silver, and bronze in 1967.

The obverse of the medal depicts the four Sovereigns of the victorious powers (George IV, then Prince Regent, Emperor Franz I of Austria, Tsar Alexander I of Russia, and Friedrich Wilhelm III of Prussia) in the centre, crowned with laurels and wearing classical drapery. Allegorical figures are shown around the rim of the medal. Apollo drives the chariot of the sun towards the constellation of Gemini (personified by Castor and Pollux) indicating June, the month of the battle. Behind Apollo are Zephyr and Iris, holding wreaths of flowers. Below Castor and Pollux is Themis, Goddess of Justice, elegantly seated on a classical throne, then the Fates and the Furies, within the Cimmerian caverns, and divided by the figure of Night riding in another chariot. As Night contrasts with Day in the composition, so does Hercules, symbolising Power, contrast with Themis (Justice), sitting at the opposite side of the medal. The meaning of the iconography is that the battle of Waterloo is the triumph of light over darkness, and of Justice over Power.

The reverse shows Wellington and Blücher riding with Victory, who guides them towards glory. Jupiter drives his chariot above them, and strikes with his thunderbolts the defeated Giants, who number nineteen, signifying the number of years the Napoleonic wars lasted.

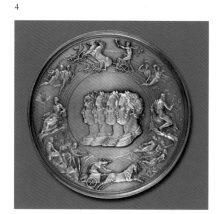

4

5 Benedetto Pistrucci (1783–1855)
Celebratory Medal for the Duke of Wellington, 1841

Bronze, diameter 61 mm
Signed on the obverse and on the reverse 'PISTRUCCI'
Fitzwilliam Museum, Cambridge
Literature: Parkes Weber, 1894, pp. 114–115, no. 189; *Mostra . . .*, 1955, p. 21, p. 79; Brown, 1987, p. 60, no. 2011; Eimer, 1987, p. 163, no. 1353; Pirzio Biroli Stefanelli, 1989, vol. I, p. 35, no.13, pp. 133–137, vol. II, nos 100–105; Marsh, 1996, p. 47, p. 100, pl. 35.

Pistrucci made the models for this work while in Rome in 1839, and displayed them the following year at the Royal Academy. The design of the classical helmet on the reverse had already been conceived in a wax model of 1825 (Rome, Museo della Zecca). The idea for a medal celebrating Wellington probably dates to that year, ten years after the Battle of Waterloo. The medal was not however struck until 1841 (it was produced in both bronze and silver), the delay being due to the fact that Pistrucci had suffered a long period of problems with his eyesight.

The obverse shows a portrait of Wellington, with the words 'FIELD MARSHAL ARTHUR DUKE OF WELLINGTON'. Pistrucci also made three cameos of the Duke, probably with the same portrait, but none of these has been located.

On the reverse there is the elegant motif of the classical helmet, with the inscription 'NOVA CANTAMUS TROPAEA AUGUST 1841' (we sing anew of our victories August 1841). A more unusual version of this medal bears another inscription on the reverse 'VIS VIRTUS VERITAS W.R.H.' (strength, virtue, truth). This is the motto of William Richard Hamilton, Pistrucci's great friend and supporter, and probably indicates it was made specifically for him.

6 Benedetto Pistrucci (1783–1855)
Celebratory Medal for William Wellesley-Pole, 3rd Earl of Mornington, 1823

Bronze, diameter 51 mm
Signed on the obverse 'PISTRUCCI'
National Portrait Gallery, London
Literature: Billing, 1875, p. 207; Parkes Weber, 1894, p. 115, no. 190; *Mostra . . .*, 1955, p. 20; Brown, 1980, p. 294, no. 1121; Pollard, 1984, p. 44, p. 51, pls 12–13; Eimer, 1987, p. 144, no. 1167; Pirzio Biroli Stefanelli, 1988, vol. I, p. 34, no. 4, p.118, vol. II, no. 74; Pirzio Biroli Stefanelli, forthcoming, vol. II, 5; Marsh, 1996, pp. 27-28, pp. 110-111 pls 45–46.

William Wellesley-Pole (1763–1845), 3rd Earl of Mornington and Baron Maryborough, was the older brother of the Duke of Wellington. He was Master of the Mint between 1814 and 1823, and was responsible for commissioning Pistrucci to produce the new coinage of George III in 1817.

The medal was made in 1823, on the occasion of Wellesley-Pole's retirement from the Mint. The reverse bears a long Latin inscription: IN HONOREM VIRI PRAENOR G V POLE/ BARON MARYBOROUGH/ REBUS MONET PER ANN IX PRAEFECTI/ QUI NUMOS BRITANN LONGO USO DETRITOS/ NON SOLUM IN PRISTINUM NITOREM RESTITUIT/ SED NOVOS SED PULCHRIORES REDDIDIT/ ET QUI IN NUMIS REMITTENDIS/ IN OMNES PARTES REGIONIS/ ED SAPIENTIA REM GESSIT/ UT UBIQUE EODEM FEDE FERE TEMPORE/ VETUS MONETA IN DESUETUDINEM ADIIT/ ATQUE IN PUBLICA COMMODA CITO NOVA SUCCESSIT/ SUMMA RATIONE AEQUITATEQUE ADHIBITA/ NUMUM HUNC/ OBSERVANT ATQUE AMICIT MONUMENTUM/ CUDE FECERUNT MONETARII/ IN OFFICINA REGIA LOND/ A S MDCCCXXIII. (In honour of the Master of the Mint, William Wellesley-Pole, Baron Maryborough, who was in charge for nine years, and who not only restored to their pristine splendour coins worn out through long use, but produced new ones, which were even more beautiful, and who in his wisdom produced coins to be sent out to all parts and regions, so that during his time whenever there were faults he withdrew old money and promoted public welfare once again. This coinage is subject to the highest reason and fairness, and this memorial is given in friendship, made by the moneyers in the Royal Mint in the year 1823).

The medal portrays one of Pistrucci's leading supporters. It was thanks to Wellesley-Pole that the Italian was given the commission for the Waterloo Medal. His departure from the Royal Mint weakened Pistrucci's position there, and was one of the causes of the artist's anxiety, culminating in the creation of the *Capriccio*.

7   Benedetto Pistrucci (1783–1855)
Bust of Samuel Cartwright, 1841

White marble, height 429 mm
Signed 'BENEDETTO PISTRUCCI ROYAL MINT'
National Portrait Gallery, London
Literature: Christie, Manson and Woods, 1865, p. 8, no. 77; Jung, 1981, p. 98, no. 4983; Pollard, 1984, p. 46, pl. 16; Pirzio Biroli Stefanelli, 1989, vol. I, p. 39, no. 14.

Samuel Cartwright (1788–1864) was a dentist, and one of the pioneers in the academic teaching of his discipline. He was appointed in 1844 as surgeon-dentist to King's College Hospital, London, and in 1860 he became the first professor of dental surgery in Great Britain. He also founded the British Odontological Society. Among his clients was the painter J. M. W. Turner. Cartwright was Pistrucci's dentist, and the artist also made for him a red jasper cameo representing Medusa, which was sold at Christie's in 1865, and is now in the Metropolitan Museum of Art in New York (accession no. 2003.431) (Pirzio Biroli Stefanelli, 1989, vol. I, p.25, no. 42). This bust is considered by many to be Pistrucci's finest portrait. Graham Pollard notes that it is 'worthy of the best British sculptor of the day, Francis Chantrey'. This is certainly true although of course Pistrucci twice refused to copy portraits by Chantrey. Interestingly Pistrucci added the phrase 'Royal Mint' to

6

7

his signature, emphasising his status, however nebulous that had become by this date.

A letter written by Nicolò Paganini dating to 1834 (Genoa, Palazzo Doria Tursi) establishes a connection between the violinist and Cartwright. Paganini (1782–1840) thanks the dentist attending to his teeth while he was in London for a concert. It was probably between 1831 and 1834 that Pistrucci portrayed Paganini in a lost bust, probably inspired by the wax portrait in the Museo della Zecca in Rome (L. Pirzio Biroli Stefanelli, 1989, vol. I, p.160–161, no. 144, vol. II, no. 144). The Palazzo Doria Tursi in Genoa owns a cameo derived from the Pistrucci wax and donated by Benito Mussolini to the city of Genoa in 1940.

8 Benedetto Pistrucci (1783–1855)

George III, 1817

Cameo in red jasper, diameter 38 mm
Signed 'PISTRUCCI'
The Royal Mint, Llantrisant
Literature: Billing, 1875, pp. 190–192, p. 201; Hocking, 1906, p. 165, no. 1804; Forrer, 1906, p. 33; Pirzio Biroli Stefanelli, 1989, vol. I, p. 29, no. 67: Marsh, 1996, p. 17, p. 68, pl. 5.

This cameo is important in the context of the first contacts between the Royal Mint and Pistrucci. Sir Joseph Banks asked Pistrucci to make a wax portrait of King George III in 1816. The artist, unable to portray the king from life, drew inspiration from a coin by the gem-engraver and medallist Nathaniel Marchant (1739–1816). Pleased with the wax, Banks commissioned a red jasper cameo from Pistrucci. When it was completed Banks introduced the Italian artist to the Master of the Mint, William Wellesley-Pole, who gave the cameo to the Chief Engraver at the Mint, Thomas Wyon (active 1796–d.1817) to be used as the basis of the design for the king's portrait on the Half-Crown. The result was disappointing,

8

and after Wyon's death in 1817, Pistrucci was put in charge of designing the new coinage with the profile of the King on the obverse and St George and the Dragon on the reverse.

The present cameo was used for the portrait of George III on the Half-Crown, one of Pistrucci's numismatic masterpieces. The use of a cameo as a model for a coin is unique, and testifies to Pistrucci's own training as a gem-engraver, and his lack of experience in the field of numismatics. But he learned quickly and taught himself to engrave the dies, in order to avoid the loss of quality that had occurred when Wyon tried to transfer the first cameo on to a coin.

The portrait of the King is much more elegant and classicising than the exemplars previously used for British coinage. Pistrucci's knowledge of Greek and Roman coins is evident in this cameo and in the coins derived from it. Three wax models relating to this royal portrait for the coinage of 1816–17 are held in the Museo della Zecca in Rome.

9 Benedetto Pistrucci (1783–1855)

Gold Sovereign, 1817

Diameter 22 mm
The Royal Mint, Llantrisant
Literature: Billing, 1875, pp. 190–192; *Mostra . . .* , 1955, p. 19; Jones, 1984, p. 136 ff.; Marsh, 1996, pp. 17–19; Clancy, 2000, pp. 118–120.

The Gold Sovereign is the first coin designed by Pistrucci for the Royal Mint, and combines two of his great innovations in British coinage: the profile portrait of George III, and St George and the Dragon. For the origins of the portrait of the King, see cat. no. 8.

According to Pistrucci, the idea for the St George and the Dragon was conceived in 1816, after Joseph Banks introduced him to Lord and Lady Spencer. Lady Spencer asked him to make a model in wax of that subject, 'in Greek style, as that was the style in which naked figures were done' (Pirzio Biroli Stefanelli 1989, I, p. 87). Later William Wellesley-Pole commissioned from Pistrucci a red jasper cameo with the scene of St George and the Dragon to be used for the reverse of the new coinage. The cameo is missing today, but it is interesting to note that Pistrucci once again used a cameo as the starting point for his design for a coin, as he had done for the George III coinage. The British Museum owns a wax model on

glass for the St George and the Dragon (Marsh 1996, p. 118, no. 53).

With this Gold Sovereign, celebrated by baron Dominique-Vivant Denon (1747–1825) as the most beautiful coin in Europe, Pistrucci introduced many innovations. He abandoned the traditional heraldic motifs in favour of the representation of St George, with the saint presented as a mythological hero. Even the antiquarian and numismatist Edward Hawkins (1789–1882), one of the staunchest critics of Pistrucci, admitted that the Gold Sovereign was a coin of great modernity, although he attacked the Royal Mint for giving the responsibility of making the new coinage to a foreigner (Pirzio Biroli Stefanelli, 1989, vol. I, p. 88).

10 Benedetto Pistrucci (1783–1855)

The Prince Regent (later King George IV)

Cameo in onyx, 40 x 35 mm
Signed 'PISTRUCCI'
Fitzwilliam Museum, Cambridge
Literature: *Mostra . . .* , 1955, p. 22; Christie's, London, 26 June 1980, lot 153; Pollard-Mauri Mori, 1981, p. 24; Pollard, 1984, p. 50, pl. 8; Pirzio Biroli Stefanelli, 1989, vol. I, p. 29, no. 72; Marsh, 1996, p.28, p. 95, pl. 30.

This cameo dates to 1817–20, and is one of the finest to be engraved by Pistrucci in England. During the Regency the Italian artist was commissioned to make some of his most renowned works, such as the Waterloo Medal, the models for the medal commemorating the acquisition of the Elgin marbles, and of course the Gold Sovereign and the new coinage. Pistrucci probably portrayed the Prince Regent from life, as he was to do on other occasions after George had ascended the throne (see cat. no. 11). The balanced image in profile shows the Prince as a classical ruler, with a diadem in the hair. The stone is cut with great

10

precision, and the effigy is in a precisely calculated low relief. A number of waxes in the Museo della Zecca in Rome show George IV, but he is represented as Prince Regent in only two of them.

11 Benedetto Pistrucci (1783–1855)
Laudatory Medal of George IV, 1824

Bronze, diameter 60 mm
Signed 'PISTRUCCI'
Fitzwilliam Museum, Cambridge
Literature: Parkes Weber, 1894, p. 115, no. 191; *Mostra . . .* , 1955, p. 20, pp. 50–51; Brown, 1980, p. 298, no. 1221; Eimer, 1987, p. 144, no. 1171; Pirzio Biroli Stefanelli, 1989, vol. I, p. 34. no. 5; Marsh, 1996, p. 28.

11

This medal was also struck in gold and in silver by Rundell, Bridge, and Rundell. It is sometimes called the Greek Medal, because of its inscriptions. It was made in 1824, and Pistrucci proudly wrote under the profile of the King that the portrait was from life. This is an important detail, because he had refused to copy a portrait by Thomas Lawrence in 1821 for the Coronation Medal, and a bust by Francis Chantrey in 1822 for the coins for the new King. The reverse shows a trident, the symbol of Neptune, which serves as an allegory of British naval power. The two dolphins derive from Sicilian coins, as Billing noted (Billing, 1875, p. 24).

12 Benedetto Pistrucci (1783–1855)
Bacchic Mask

Cameo in onyx, 52 x 44 mm
Private Collection
Literature: Sotheby's London, 7 February 1859, lot 2553; Billing, 1875, p. 207, p. 210; Forrer, 1906, p. 32; Maesta' di Roma, 2003, cat. no. XI.1.35; *Mostra . . .* , 1955, p. 24; Pollard, 1984, pl. 1; Pirzio Biroli Stefanelli 1989, I, p. 24, no. 37, pl. 49b.

12

This cameo relates to a wax in the Museo della Zecca in Rome (Pirzio Biroli Stefanelli, 1989, vol. I, p. 216, no. 318; vol. II, no. 318). The date of the cameo is in some dispute. According to Pollard it may have been made by Pistrucci in Rome around 1812 for the dealer Angelo Bonelli, and then sold to William Beckford as a Greek original. However Pirzio Biroli Stefanelli quotes a passage from Archibald Billing's fragmentary autobiography of Pistrucci (pp. 207, 210) from which it appears that the cameo was made in Old Windsor, and therefore after 1844.

13 Carl Friedrich Voigt (1800–1874)
Portrait of Benedetto Pistrucci, 1826

Gilt bronze medal, diameter 86 mm
Royal Mint, Llantrisant
Literature: Forrer 1916, VI, pp. 305–10; Marsh, 1996, pp. 29–32, pp. 82–83, pls 17–18.

Voigt, a native of Berlin, joined the Royal Mint in 1825 as a pupil of Pistrucci, and stayed in London for about a year. He had already made some medals in Germany, but benefited professionally from his time at the Mint.

The medal is relatively rare, and represents Pistrucci at the age of 43, in profile, with the words 'BENEDETTO PISTRUCCI STEIN – UND STEMPELSCHNEIDER' (Benedetto Pistrucci, gem-carver and die-sinker). Few portraits of Pistrucci exist. He produced a self-portrait bust, which is sadly untraced and known only through copies. The other self-portrait by Pistrucci is the full-length nude in wax in the Museo della Zecca representing himself as Atlas which was then reproduced in the *Capriccio*. There are in addition two paintings by Busiri (both painted in Rome in 1839), and a photograph

taken by W.R. Hamilton in 1853 in London. The identification of the subject of a cameo in the Victoria and Albert Museum as Pistrucci (inv. no. A.5-1940) is questioned by Pirzio Biroli Stefanelli (1989, vol. I, p.40, no. 6).

14 Maria Elisa Pistrucci (1824–1881)
Medallion with the heads of Flora and Ceres

Marble, diameter 230 mm
Signed on the edge 'M. E. Pistrucci'
Private Collection
Literature: unpublished.

Very little is known about Pistrucci's sons and daughters, except for Camillo. Maria Elisa and Elena remained in England with their father until his death. The forthcoming publication of the third volume of studies by Lucia Pirzio Biroli Stefanelli will bring to the attention of scholars a large number of unpublished letters and documents that will certainly add to our knowledge of them. This medallion is particularly interesting because it is one of the very few known works by Maria Elisa, who also engraved cameos. The Flora is a copy of one of the medallions on top of the *Capriccio*, while the Ceres derives from a wax by Benedetto Pistrucci in the Museo della Zecca in Rome (Pirzio Biroli Stefanelli, 1989, vol. I, p. 223, no. 332; vol. II, no. 332).

ACKNOWLEDGMENTS

The author would like to thank Philip Attwood, Piero Boccardo, Andrew Ciechanowiecki, Kevin Clancy, Alex Corney, Alberto Di Castro, Alessandra Di Castro, Graham P. Dyer, Alvar González-Palacios, Ben Hanly, Tim Knox, Mark Jones, Alan Irvine, Kate Mayne, William Palin, Andreas Pampoulides, Lucia Pirzio Biroli Stefanelli, Pippa Shirley, Andrea Sommariva, Timothy Stevens, Marjorie Trusted, Philip Ward-Jackson, Robert Wenley, and Paul Williamson.

Without their help, advice, and patience, this work would have not been possible.

CATALOGUE

OF THE

UNFINISHED WORKS, IN MARBLE,

MOULDS, CASTS,

Valuable Lathes and Tools,

OF THAT DISTINGUISHED ARTIST, THE LATE

SIGNOR PISTRUCCI,

HER MAJESTY'S MEDALLIST,

INCLUDING

A BEAUTIFUL MODEL OF A MAGDALEN,

With the Work partly executed in Marble,

Antique Fragments, Moulds, Models, Dies of Medals, Eight Blocks of Parian and Carrara Marble,

A DIE SINKER'S LATHE, OR TOUR-LE-PORTRAIT,

By PANISSET, with additional Mechanism by Sig. PISTRUCCI,

SCULPTOR'S BENCHES,

WITH RISING SCREWS, OF GREAT POWER,

Work Benches, Tools, and Miscellaneous Effects.

Removed from ENGLEFIELD GREEN.

WHICH WILL BE SOLD BY AUCTION,

BY

Messrs. FOSTER & SON

At the Gallery, 54, Pall Mall,

On FRIDAY, 30th of NOVEMBER, 1855,

AT TWELVE FOR ONE O'CLOCK.

On View Two Days prior—the Sculpture, Lathes, &c. at the Gallery, 54, Pall Mall, and the Marbles, Benches, &c. at Mr. KELLY's Premises, William and Mary Yard, Great Pulteney Street, Golden Square. Catalogues at Messrs. FOSTER's Offices, 54, Pall Mall.

LOT

1   The iron-work for a marble saw, 10 mallets, marble polishing tools, an iron bust stand, 12 large rasps, 12 files, and 3 soldering irons

2   Two hundred and ninety-six marble chisels

3   Three iron points, 2 hooks for pointing busts, 9 copper and brass tools, 6 wooden tools, and a quantity of pomice stones

4   Three hundred and nine rasps and files for marble, 2 small marble saws, 8 long tools for working in plaster, a lamp, and a quantity of type metal

5   One hundred and twelve marble chisels

6   Eighteen iron chipping mallets and a mallet

7   Four wooden stands, 2 carpenter's tools for making lines (one in brass and one in wood), a parallel rule, a 2 ft. rule, a 1 ft. ditto, and a carpenter's rule

8   A saw set, a wooden scraper, a bright hammer, a pair of scissors, 2 blow pipes, 2 drills, a plumb line, an axe, 2 saws, a key hole saw with six blades, an iron saw and frame, a screw driver, a bed wrench, a screw hammer, a key hole saw, and 4 steel squares

9   2 pairs of wire scissors, 5 pairs of pincers, 2 tools (bookbinder's), a vice, a screw plate with 12 plates, 3 scrapers with handles, a screw plate with 12 plates, a ditto, and a polishing hammer

10   A tool for turning screws, an iron stock, 2 iron handles, a crow bar, 42 files, 3 pieces of iron for vice, 3 panel saws, a large saw and frame, and 14 rasps

11   A large ebony and iron compass, 5 bows for drills, a wood and brass compass, a drill with 15 points, 22 rimers, a large steel and wood square, and a pair of callipers

12   Eight brass compasses, 2 iron ditto, 5 keys for compasses, 2 drills with 24 points, and a drill

13   A compass with 6 points, a wooden stand for drill points, a large square stand for grinding chisels, a stamping tool, 2 large saws, and [crossed through]

14   Two small saws with frame, a level, a large iron calliper, 2 cheeks, 3 burnishing tools, 2 keys for compasses, 20 drill points, 2 walnut-tree trays, a piece of mahogany, 11 file handles, and 5 small models

15   Two sculptor's modelling frames, quantity of modelling tools, furnace tongs, and 9 large crow bars

16   A large oak modelling bench, an oak revolving ditto, and 2 small modelling benches

17   A plane with 8 points, and 9 other planes

18   Four planes with steel beds, and a steel plane for planning brass

19   Nineteen chisels (carpenter's), 8 gimblets, 6 brad-awls, a mallet with iron frame, a stock with 37 bits, and a ditto with 41 bits

20   Eight iron die pots and 11 furnace irons

21   A block of fine PARIAN MARBLE, 2 ft. 10 by 2 ft., 5 ft. long

22   A block of CARRARA marble, 3 ft. 3 by 2 ft., 1 ft. 7 deep

23   A ditto, 3 ft. by 1ft. 4, 6 in. deep

24   A ditto, 2 ft. by 1 ft. 4, 10 in.

25   A ditto, 2 ft. 2 by 2 ft., 11 in. deep

26   A triangular ditto, 2 ft. 4 by 1 ft. 3, average 15 in., for a bust

27   A block, 2 ft. by 1 ft. 3, 11 ins

28   A ditto, 3 ft. by 1 ft. 11, 7 in. thick

29   Five [altered to 8] smaller pieces and small marble truck

30   A sculptor's modelling round bench with strong iron revolving top

31   Five iron mould frames, 4 screws, crucibles, and 6 iron clay standards

32   A large screw press for gutta percha

33   A 4 ft. 6 wainscot bench with drawers and a bench for modelling tools

34 A 6 ft. square wainscot bench, with revolving frame, for modelling from the life

35 A slate sketching slab, 6 ft. 4 by 3 ft.

36 A large modelling bench with revolving frame

37 A ditto

38 A small lathe for grinding sculptors' tools

39 A SCULPTOR'S LARGE IRON-BOUND MARBLE BENCH, WITH A THREE-SCREW POWER TO RAISE SIX TONS, designed by and manufactured under the superintendence of the late Signor Pistrucci

40 A small ditto with one screw

41 A DITTO CLAY-MODELLING BENCH, with screws, rising top, and original arrangement for the steps

42 A VALUABLE TOUR-LE-PORTRAIT, OR DIE-SINKING AND MEDAL LATHE, BY PANISSET OF PARIS, WITH ADDITIONAL MECHANISM AND IMPROVEMENTS BY THE LATE SIGNOR PISTRUCCI, for making large or small dies, medals or coins, by the hand or foot

43 A STEEL WORKER'S solid mahogany BENCH, with 2 pedestals of 9 drawers

44 A ditto with 14 drawers

45 A large steel die dish and stand

46 A ditto with lead stand

47 A large brass die dish [crossed through: and a leather sand cushion]

48 A mahogany work bench with a large iron vice

49 A fragment of an ANTIQUE GREEK marble bust, and a mould from it

50 A MOULD of the late Signor Pistrucci's fine colossal bust of the late Duke of Wellington

51 A ditto of Signor Pistrucci's bust of Paganini

52 A ditto of Madame PASTA

53 Two moulds of female heads and a ditto of an antique head

54 A mould of a pedestal, and a plaster model of a thistle

55 A mould of the late Mr. Pistrucci's beautiful work, in the possession of the Right Hon. Henry Labouchere, known as the Capriccio

56 A mould, by the late Mr. Pistrucci, of the bust of the Princess Dahomy

57 An original model for a fountain, and a mould of a fountain, incomplete

58 A small bust in plaster of the late Duke of Wellington, a plaster cast, a torso of Venus, and a ditto of a shell ornament

59 An original model of a female figure of Thetis, designed for supporting classical drapery

60 An original model for a candelabrum, prepared for the Marquis of Abercorn

61 A ditto, sketch in plaster for the Nelson monument, and a model in plaster for ditto

62 A ditto, sketch for the Coronation Medal, The Queen on the Throne, with allegorical figures

63 A ditto, whole length figure of King George IV

64 An original plaster basso relieve, by the late Signor Pistrucci, subject, Achilles and Thetis, 6 ft. 6 by 4 ft. 6

65 A copy, in plaster, of the preceding by Mr. R. Pistrucci

66 A cast from the Elgin marbles, The recumbent figure of Theseus

67 A ditto

68 A ditto, a Horse's Head

69 A cast from a basso relieve in the Capitol, and a ditto from the Elgin marbles

70 A ditto, from the antique

71 An antique Greek marble cuirass, from Athens

72 Dies for the medal of George IV. – 3 of the head, 1 punch, raised, 3 preparatory dies, 3 matrixes of the reverse, 1 die, 1 punch, and the die, imperfect

73 Medal of the Duke of York. – 3 dies of the head, 2 punches, 2 matrixes, 1 die of the reverse with inscription, and 1 plain for ditto

74 Medal of the Duke of Wellington. – 1 punch of the head, 2 matrixes, 1 die, 1 die of the reverse with helmet, 2 matrixes of the reverse, 2 ditto, not finished, 2 punches, finished and 1 ditto not finished

75 A large plain die, a ditto with inscription for Paganini's bust, unfinished

76 A ditto, unfinished

77 A large punch with head of Sir Gilbert Blain, and a ditto in copper

78 A die with a front face, and 13 incomplete and finished dies

Unfinished Works of the late Signor PISTRUCCI

79 A BUST, in marble, of Count Pozzo di Borgo, and mould

80 A shell ornament, in marble, with the plaster cast

81 A marble bust of a lady

82 A BEAUTIFUL MODEL OF A MAGDALEN, BY THE LATE SIGNOR PISTRUCCI, with the work partly executed in CARRARA MARBLE

83 TWO CAPITAL DOUBLE BARREL GUNS, BY ERIN EPAGE OF PARIS, with percussion locks and numerous apparatus, in case

84 A blunderbuss, a pair of pistols, 2 shot belts and 2 powder flasks

BIBLIOGRAPHY

1830 *Gentleman's Magazine*, C, Part I, p. 543;

1837–1838 *A collection of letters etc. from newspapers and magazines, on the respective merits of B. Pistrucci and W. Wyon as medallists*, London (British Library, Rare Books)

1838–1839 Cautus, Cast-dies for Medals, in *Numismatic Chronicle*, pp. 122–127; J. W. B., Pistrucci's Invention: a letter to the Editor, in *Numismatic Chronicle*, pp. 53–62; W. R. Hamilton, Cast-dies for Medals, in *Numismatic Chronicle*, pp. 230–232

1839 *The Literary Gazette*, p. 39

1849 *The Art Journal*, November; Report of the Commissioners appointed to enquire into the constitution, management and expense of the Royal Mint, London, pp. 207–211

1849–1850 Mr. Pistrucci on the Waterloo Medal. Notes and observations of Benedetto Pistrucci on the best mode of hardening the Matrices of the Waterloo Medal and also on other mechanical operations which will be required for the successful striking of the Medals, in *Numismatic Chronicle*, XII, pp. 115–122

1854 L. Waagen, *Treasures of Art in Great Britain*, II, London

1855 Catalogue of the Unfinished Works in Marble, Moulds, Casts, valuable Lathes and Tools, of that distinguished artist, the late Signor Pistrucci, Her Majesty's Medallist, Foster & Son, 30 November 1855; *Illustrated London News*, 22 September, p. 347

1856 Atti della Pontificia Accademia Bolognese di Belle Arti per la distribuzione dei premi dell' anno 1856, pp. 46–47, pp. 51–59; *Gentleman's Magazine*, XLV, pp. 653–656; *The Art Journal*, II, p. 27

1861 Pistrucci's large Waterloo Medal, in *Illustrated London News*, 22 June

1865 Catalogue of the valuable collection of oriental, Dresden, Sevres, and Chelsea porcelain, carvings in ivory, snuff-boxes, bronzes, marbles, clocks and other decorative objects formed by that well-known Amateur Samuel Cartwright Esq., F.R.S., Christie, Manson and Woods, 28 February 1865; I. Ciampi, Benedetto Pistrucci, in *Arti e Lettere*, II, pp. 329–338

1866 C. W. King, *Handbook of Engraved Gems*, London, pp. 131–132

1867 A. Billing, *The science of Gems, Jewels, Coins and Medals, Ancient and Modern*, London

1872 C. W. King, *Antique gems and rings*, London, p. 34, pp. 448–451

1875 A. Billing, *The science of Gems, Jewels, Coins and Medals, Ancient and Modern*, 2nd edition, London

1881 H. A. Grueber, *Guide to English Medals*, London

1884 R. L. Kenyon, *The gold coins of England*, London, pp. 197–199, pp. 200–202, p. 206

1887 F. Azzurri, *Cenni biografici di Benedetto Pistrucci letti nelle sale dell' insigne Accademia di San Luca il 21 aprile 1887*, Rome

1888 Roma, Ricordi di Benedetto Pistrucci, in *Arte e Storia*, VIII, p. 64

1890 I. Ciampi, Benedetto Pistrucci incisore, in *Vite di Romani illustri*, III, 1890

1894 F. Parkes Weber, Medals and medallions of the nineteenth century relating to England by foreign artists, in *Numismatic Chronicle*, XIV, pp. 112–117

1897 H. Jouin, La sculpture dans les cimitières de Paris, le Père-Lachaise, in *Nouvelles Archives de l'Art Français*, XIII, p. 196

1904 F. Lenzi, *L'arte e le opere di Benedetto Pistrucci: un'altra collezione che forse se ne va*, Orbetello

1906 L. Forrer, Benedetto Pistrucci Italian Medallist & Gem-engraver, Extract from the *Biographical Dictionary of Medallists*, London; W. J. Hocking, *Catalogue of coins, tokens, medals, dies and seals in the museum of the Royal Mint*, London, II, pp. 207–210

1916 O. M. Dalton, *Catalogue of the engraved gems of the post-classical period in the British Museum*, London, pp. LIV–LV

1921 L. Pratesi, Nel primo centenario della morte di Napoleone I: una medaglia che non fu mai coniata, in *Arte e Storia*, VI, XL, pp. 91–59

1931 C. Oman, *The Coinage of England*, Oxford, pp. 366, pp. 369–371

1932–1933 G. C. Brooke, Pistrucci's model of the St. George for the Sovereign, in *The British Museum Quarterly*, VII, pp. 52–53

1941 Cenni sulla vita e sulle opere di Benedetto Pistrucci, in *Ministero delle Finanze, Relazione della Regia Zecca, esercizi 1914–1933*, pp. 161–251

1952 L. Jannattoni, Una famiglia romana: i Pistrucci, in *Strenna dei Romanisti*, XIII, pp. 223–229

1955 *Mostra di Benedetto Pistrucci (1784–1855)*, Rome, Palazzo Braschi

1962 R. Gunnis, *Dictionary of British Sculptors, 1660–1851*, London, pp. 306–307

1964 G. Hubert, *Les sculpteurs italiens en France sous la révolution, l'empire, et la restauration 1790–1830*, Paris, p. 161

1966 A. Busiri Vici, Un ritratto inedito di Benedetto Pistrucci, in *Strenna dei Romanisti*, XXVIII, pp. 69–73

1968 *Royal Academy of Arts Bicentenary Exhibition, 1768–1968*, London, vol. I, p. 244, vol. II, p. 101

1969 R. Davies, Benedetto Pistrucci and the British Crown, in *Coins and Medals*, March, p. 200

1970 A. Graves, *The Royal Academy of Arts. A complete dictionary of contributors and their work from its foundation in 1769 to 1904*, vol. III, London

1971 J. G. Pollard, Matthew Boulton and the reducing machine in England, in *The Numismatic Chronicle*, XI, pp. 311–317

1972 M. Valeriani, *Arte della medaglia in Italia*, Rome, pp. 35–40

1973 H. M. Colvin, *The history of the King's works*, VI, 1782–1851, London, p. 452, n.5

1975 C. Avery, Neo-classical portraits by Pistrucci and Rauch, in *Apollo*, CII, pp. 36–43

1978 J. Kent, *2000 Years of British Coins*, London, pp. 58–61

1979 G. Incisa Della Rocchetta, *La collezione dei ritratti dell' Accademia di San Luca in Roma*, Rome, p. 69, p. 205; M. Jones, *The Art of the Medal*, London, pp. 102–105

1980 L. Brown, *A Catalogue of British Historical Medals, 1760–1960, I, The Accession of George III to the Death of William IV*, London, pp. 208–212, no. 870, pp. 263–264, nos 1069–1070, p. 294, no. 1211, p. 298, no. 1221, p. 307, no. 1258, p. 314, nos 1283–1284, p. 348, no. 1439; M. A. Marsh, *The Gold Sovereign, the Gold Half Sovereign*, Cambridge

1981 J. G. Pollard-G. Mauri Mori, *Medaglie e monete*, Milan, pp. 23–24, p. 75; H. Wollaston, *British Official Medals for Coronations and Jubilees*, Nottingham, pp. 24–26

1982 M. Clarke-N. Penny, *The Arrogant Connoisseur: Richard Payne Knight 1751–1824*, Manchester, pp. 74–75, p. 128

1984 S. Balbi De Caro, Il Gabinetto Numismatico della Zecca: breve storia di una collezione di prestigio, in *Bollettino di Numismatica*, I, pp. 11–26; J. G. Pollard, Benedetto Pistrucci in Inghilterra, in *La Medaglia Neoclassica in Italia e in Europa, Atti del Quarto Convegno Internazionale di Studio sulla Storia*

della Medaglia, Udine, 20–23 June 1981, pp. 37–54; M. Jones, The life and work of William Wyon, in in *La Medaglia Neoclassica in Italia e in Europa, Atti del Quarto Convegno Internazionale di Studio sulla Storia della Medaglia*, Udine, 20–23 June 1981, pp. 119–140; M. Jones, The Fothergillian Medal of the Royal Humane Society, in *The British Numismatic Journal*, LIV, pp. 248–262; L. Pirzio Biroli Stefanelli, Benedetto Pistrucci (Roma, 1784–Englefield Green 1855): tre cere inedite del Museo di Roma, in *Bollettino dei Musei Comunali di Roma*, XXXI, pp. 92–96

1985 G. K. Beulah, Pistrucci's great Waterloo Medal, in *The Medal*, 7, pp. 12–14

1986 G. P. Dyer, *The Royal Mint, An Illustrated History*, Caerphilly, p. 29

1987 L. Brown, *A Catalogue of British Historical Medals, 1837–1901, The Reign of Queen Victoria*, London, pp. 14–15, nos. 1801–1802, p. 57, no. 2000, p. 60, no. 2011, p. 182, no. 2156; C. Eimer, *British Commemorative Medals and their values*, London, p. 133, no. 1067, p. 142, no. 1146, p. 144, nos 1167, 1171, p. 145, no. 1184, p. 146, no. 1189, p. 150, no. 1230, p. 158, no. 1309, p. 159, no. 1315, p. 163, no. 1353; C. M. Mancini, Conversazione sulla Sovrana, in *ARRO, Quaderni*, I, p. 9 ff.; I. S. Weber, Bacchus und Manade. Unpublizierte Kameen des Benedetto Pistrucci in der Staatliche Munzsammlung München, in *Weltkunst*, LVII, 23, pp. 3583–3585

1988 L. Pirzio Biroli Stefanelli, un incisore romano a Londra: Benedetto Pistrucci capo medaglista di Sua Maesta', in *AIAM, VII mostra della medaglia e placchetta d'arte*, Rome, pp. 37–45

1989 G. P. Dyer, *Royal Sovereign, 1489–1989, III, The Modern Sovereign*, London, 1989; L. Pirzio Biroli Stefanelli, *I modelli in cera di Benedetto Pistrucci, Bollettino di Numismatica, Monografia*, (2 vols.), Rome

1990 L. Pirzio Biroli Stefanelli, Un cammeo inedito di Benedetto Pistrucci, in *Bollettino Numismatico*, VIII, I, pp. 14–15

1992 C. E. Challis, *A new history of the Royal Mint*, Cambridge

1995 L. Pirzio Biroli Stefanelli, Nove modelli inediti di Benedetto Pistrucci, in *Bollettino di Numismatica*, 25, pp. 251–156; L. Pirzio Biroli Stefanelli, *Opere di Benedetto Pistrucci nel Museo di Roma*.

1996 M. A. Marsh, *Benedetto Pistrucci. Principal Engraver and Chief Medallist of the Royal Mint*, Hardwick

1997 S. Balbi De Caro, Benedetto Pistrucci e l'arte di modellare in cera, in *La tradizione classica nella medaglia d'arte dal Rinascimento al neoclassico, Atti della convegno internazionale*, Udine, pp. 116–124

1998 L. Pirzio Biroli Stefanelli, Breve nota in margine al restauro dei modelli in cera di Benedetto Pistrucci nel Museo di Roma, in *Bolettino dei Musei Comunali di Roma*, XII, pp. 159–161; M. Duchamp, Numismatique et Glyptique. Les soeurs de Napoleon. Pistrucci et Mastini, in *Medal*, London, no. 32, pp. 44–49

2000 K. Clancy, The reducing machine and the last coinage of George III, in *The British Numismatic Journal*, vol. LXX, pp. 118–123; L. Pirzio Biroli Stefanelli, Di Camillo Pistrucci scultore romano (1811–1854), in *La Strenna dei Romanisti*, 2000, pp. 411–424

2003 L. Pirzio Biroli Stefanelli, Nuovi documenti per Benedetto Pistrucci, in *Bollettino dei Musei Comunali di Roma*, XVII, pp. 225–228

2004 J. G. Pollard, Benedetto Pistrucci, in *Dictionary of National Biography*